DREAMWORKS
DRAGONS
RESCUE RIDERS
DRAGON DAY!

Adapted by Tina Gallo

Ready-to-Read

Simon Spotlight
New York   London   Toronto   Sydney   New Delhi

SIMON SPOTLIGHT
An imprint of Simon & Schuster Children's Publishing Division
1230 Avenue of the Americas, New York, New York 10020
This Simon Spotlight edition August 2020
DreamWorks Dragons © 2020 by DreamWorks Animation LLC. All Rights Reserved.
All rights reserved, including the right of reproduction in whole or in part in any form.
SIMON SPOTLIGHT, READY-TO-READ, and colophon are registered trademarks of
Simon & Schuster, Inc.
For information about special discounts for bulk purchases, please contact
Simon & Schuster Special Sales at 1-866-506-1949 or business@simonandschuster.com.
Manufactured in the United States of America 0720 LAK
10 9 8 7 6 5 4 3 2 1
ISBN 978-1-5344-7413-0 (hc)
ISBN 978-1-5344-7412-3 (pbk)
ISBN 978-1-5344-7414-7 (eBook)

The Rescue Riders are a team of humans and dragons. They help anyone in danger.

One day their friend Finngard
was stuck in a tree.
He needed help.

The fire fury dragon Aggro
flew up and saved Finngard!
Finngard was excited to
be saved by a dragon.

Finngard loved dragons
so much that he had made
a book of dragon drawings.

His mom showed the book
to the Rescue Riders.

The Rescue Riders decided
to have a special Dragon Day
for Finngard.

They wanted to show him
their skills so he could
add more to his book.
Aggro promised Finngard she
would come to Dragon Day.

The night before
Dragon Day,
two new dragons
arrived!

Their names were
Laburn and Cinda.
They were
fire fury dragons
just like Aggro.

Laburn and Cinda
wanted Aggro to play
with them.

The three dragons played
together all night.
They lit up the sky with
their fire blasts!

The next morning
it was Dragon Day!
Burple went first.

He rolled up in a ball and
knocked down barrels!
He was very strong.

Cutter cut wood with
his sharp tail.

Winger and Dak flew
super fast.

Summer put out a fire
with her water blast!

Aggro was not there.
She was with her new friends.

Finngard waited and waited
for Aggro to come to
Dragon Day.
Aggro did not come!
Finngard was sad.

Laburn and Cinda had asked
Aggro to come with them to
see Boiling Springs Valley.

Finngard went to the
valley too.
He was looking for Aggro.

Finngard did not know the
water in the valley was hot.
He was in danger!
Aggro saw Finngard
and saved him!

Aggro went back to
the valley to get her friends.
The dragons tried to leave,
but they got stuck in mud.

They used their fire blasts
to let the Rescue Riders
know they needed help!

The Rescue Riders saw the
fire blasts.

The Rescue Riders helped
the dragons get out of
the mud!

Aggro was sorry she missed Dragon Day, so she did something special for Finngard.

She made a drawing
of Finngard with fire!
Finngard loved it!

It was the best
Dragon Day ever!